The Shelter
Puppy

The Shelter Puppy

by Holly Webb

Illustrated by Sophy Williams

tiger tales

For everyone who works with rescued greyhounds—
you are wonderful!

tiger tales

5 River Road, Suite 128, Wilton, CT 06897
Published in the United States 2022
Originally published in Great Britain 2018
by the Little Tiger Group
Text copyright © 2018 Holly Webb
Illustrations copyright © 2018 Sophy Williams
ISBN-13: 978-1-6643-4003-9
ISBN-10: 1-6643-4003-3
Printed in the China
STP/1800/0436/1121
10 9 8 7 6 5 4 3 2 1

www.tigertalesbooks.com

Contents

Chapter One
The Perfect Idea

Caitlin twirled the end of her ponytail around her finger and tugged at it. She always did that when she was worried. Everyone else in class sounded really excited about coming up with ideas for a charity for her school's Community Week, but she wasn't. She couldn't think of *anything*. Her friend Lily was so enthusiastic that she was waving her hands around and talking so fast, Caitlin could hardly understand the words.

"The stables where I go riding! We could help them! They're part of this Riding for the Disabled charity, and so many people go there. I even helped last week. It was awesome! Sometimes it's children who are usually in a wheelchair, but they give them special saddles and it's so amazing to watch. It even seems like the horses know to be careful."

Caitlin nodded. That did sound pretty amazing. In fact, it was obviously a fabulous idea. She gave a tiny sigh. Everyone had been asked to think of a charity that the school might like to support. They were supposed to find out about the charity as their homework over the next two weekends and present the idea to their class. Then each class would vote for their favorite, and the teachers would make the final choice. But that meant *she* had to think of a charity, and she didn't know where to start.

Of course, she'd heard of the ASPCA and Guide Dogs for the Blind. But James, who sat at the next table, was already talking about guide dogs and how his next-door neighbors took care of guide dog puppies, and they had to learn that they weren't allowed to chase his cat. So that was no good....

Caitlin smiled and nodded at Lily, but she wasn't actually listening to her

friend going on about the ponies at
the riding school anymore. She was
thinking about having to stand up
in front of the class and talk. Caitlin
wasn't looking forward to it one bit.
She didn't like people staring at her.
Miss Lewis was always telling her
that she had to talk more in class, but
Caitlin tried her best not to. What if
she said something silly and everyone
laughed?

Caitlin glanced around—everyone was talking at once, and the classroom was buzzing. It was as if every single person there had an idea except for her. Even Sam Marsh, who never did any homework and had pretended that he had a sprained wrist and couldn't write for two whole days last week, was bouncing up and down in his chair. He was telling all of his friends about his fantastic plan. It had something to do with the charity his soccer team supported, which sent soccer balls and sports equipment to children in Africa.

Miss Lewis was having a very serious-sounding talk with Amy and Tayla about the hospice where Amy's grandma was being taken care of and where Tayla's mom worked as a nurse, saying of course they could do it together.

Maybe she could share Lily's riding charity, Caitlin wondered. But that wouldn't really be fair—it was Lily's idea.

"So what do you think you'll do?" Lily asked, finally running out of wonderful ponies to tell Caitlin about.

"I don't know yet…," Caitlin mumbled vaguely. "I guess I'll think of something. Maybe an animal charity."

Lily nodded enthusiastically. "I read about a donkey sanctuary in my animal magazine. You could choose that."

"Mmm." Caitlin looked down, fiddling with the pencils on the table in front of her. She *did* like the sound of

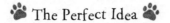

the donkey sanctuary, but she wanted to think of something for herself.

"Why do you have the car?" Caitlin looked at her mom in surprise. They usually walked home from school—it only took about 15 minutes, and it wasn't as if it were raining.

Caitlin's mom rolled her eyes, but she was smiling. "I can't believe you forgot! We're going to see Alice and Sean's new kitten, remember?"

"Oh!" Caitlin brightened. She had completely forgotten. Mom had told her at breakfast, but worrying about the charity thing at school had sent it right out of her head.

Alice and Sean were her cousins, and they had just gotten a beautiful kitten. Mom had shown Caitlin the photos that Aunt Jen had sent of a black-and-white kitten curled up on Alice's lap. He was incredibly cute.

Caitlin sped up, hurrying to the car. Aunt Jen had said that the kitten was friendly, too, and she was hoping that she would be able to cuddle him.

Her cousin Sean answered the door, with the kitten clinging for dear life onto the shoulder of his school sweater. He was the same age as Caitlin, but he went to a different school, closer to their house. "Hi, Caitlin. Hi, Aunt Sam! This is Ollie."

"Awww! He's so sweet…," Caitlin said admiringly.

"I think he's trying to get out into the yard, Sean," Caitlin's mom pointed out as the kitten started to scramble down the front of Sean's sweater. "Should we come in and shut the door?"

Sean scooped up the kitten and snuggled him. "Yes, quickly, please! He tries to get everywhere—he's so nosy. He'd love to get out to the front of the house, but he's not allowed to yet."

Caitlin's mom closed the door hurriedly, and the kitten peered curiously at Caitlin around Sean's hands. His eyes were golden yellow and very round.

"Can I pet him?" Caitlin asked hopefully, and Sean nodded.

"Sure. He's really friendly." Sean moved his fingers so that Caitlin could pet the black-and-white kitten, and Caitlin rubbed gently around his silky ears and tickled under his white chin.

"He's so soft!" she whispered delightedly as the kitten stretched out his neck, pointing his nose up to the ceiling and closing his eyes.

"He loves being scratched under the chin," Sean said. "He'll sit for a long time if you do that."

Sean's little sister came bouncing down the stairs to hug Caitlin. "Did you see our kitten?" she demanded excitedly, and Sean sighed.

"Of course she did! She's petting him right now!"

Alice stuck out her lip, and Caitlin broke in hurriedly. She loved being at Alice and Sean's house, but sometimes she went home feeling glad that her brother was so much older than she was. It meant that they didn't fight as often as Alice and Sean. It was embarrassing when Aunt Jen had to scold her cousins.

"I love Ollie. He's really cute," said Caitlin, trying to distract them. "Does he have any cat toys? Can we play with them?" she asked Alice, and her little cousin grabbed her hand and pulled her into the kitchen. Sean came after them with Ollie.

"This is his favorite! It has catnip

in it." Alice picked up a tiny stuffed mouse with a long tail made of feathers, and Ollie wriggled wildly in Sean's arms, eager to get to the mouse.

It was while they were eating dinner (with Ollie trying to climb up everyone's legs to get to the fish sticks, and Caitlin, Sean, and Alice all feeding him pieces when Caitlin's mom and Aunt Jen weren't looking) that Caitlin had her wonderful idea.

"Where did you get Ollie?" Mom asked Aunt Jen. "Was it an ad in the newspaper or something?"

Aunt Jen shook her head. "No, we went to the animal rescue center. The one next to Garland Park—you know where I mean?"

"Oh! I thought they only took in dogs."

"No, cats, too. They even had some guinea pigs. I don't think they usually have them, but someone left them outside the rescue, and they couldn't find anywhere else that would take them."

"They were so sweet!" Alice put in. "They made this little noise like *eeeep, eeeep*!"

"We loved the dogs, too, but with me

working, we simply can't have one. Ollie won't mind having the house to himself for some of the day, and it won't be long before he can go outside. We're going to put in a cat flap for him." Aunt Jen sighed. "The rescue center manager was telling me that they're struggling at the moment, actually—they're swamped with abandoned dogs that their owners couldn't take care of. And the rescue is full all the time. They'd really like to build some more dog pens in the back, but they can't afford it. They need to do some fundraising—not that they don't do a lot already. Extra fundraising, I mean. I thought I might offer to help them organize a rummage sale, or something. Maybe a sponsored walk?"

Caitlin let out a squeak of excitement, and Aunt Jen leaned over worriedly. "Caitlin, what's the matter, sweetie? Did your dinner go down the wrong way?"

Caitlin beamed at her. "Nothing's the matter. In fact, everything's perfect!"

The puppy leaped up hopefully, scratching at the wire. One of the girls who brought the food had walked past the door of the pen. It wasn't that he was hungry—he'd been fed, and he'd even left some of his dinner. He just wanted … someone.

He wanted someone to pull on the

other end of his rope toy or race him up and down the yard. Or maybe someone to squabble with about who got to have the best ball. And then he wanted someone to snuggle up with in his basket. It was too big for him by himself, even with the old teddy bear and the scruffy blanket.

But there wasn't anyone else. He was all alone, and he hated it.

Chapter Two
A Trip to the Rescue

"I think it's a great idea, Caitlin. The thing is, I don't see when we're going to be able to get there...." Caitlin's dad looked at her apologetically. "I have to help your grandma this weekend—she wants her kitchen painted—and your mom is working."

"Oh...." Caitlin stirred her cereal. She really wanted to go and visit the rescue center—of course they had a website, but it wasn't the same. She wanted her speech for the class to be good, and it wouldn't be if she hadn't actually seen the place that she was talking about. She wanted to take pictures, too. She had her camera, and she could print them out and hold them up for everyone to see.

"I'll do it." Aidan shoved his plate in the dishwasher and grabbed his bag. "See you later." He had to leave for school earlier than Caitlin because the high school was a lot farther away.

"Hey, wait! What?" Caitlin yelped.

"I'll take you there. Tomorrow. We can go on our bikes, okay? Sounds fun. But it's Saturday, so it'll have to be after soccer practice."

He disappeared into the hallway, leaving Caitlin staring after him, until she suddenly remembered to yell, "Thanks, Aidan!" as he was going out the front door.

"Aidan doesn't even like dogs or cats!" Caitlin said to Dad in surprise as the door slammed.

"It's not that he doesn't like them." Her dad shook his head. "It's just that he always had small pets. They're easier to take care of. It was too much for us to have a dog or a cat in the house when you were little."

Caitlin nodded thoughtfully. Aidan had two big cages in his bedroom now—one for his elderly rat, Trevor, and one for a whole tribe of gerbils. He loved them, and Caitlin thought they were cute, but just a little too wriggly.

You really can't cuddle with a gerbil, she thought. Not like Ollie yesterday. He'd snuggled up on her lap while she watched a Disney movie with Alice, and he'd even purred. She smiled to herself. If they went to the rescue center, maybe there would be some more kittens there. A beautiful, fluffy kitten, just like Ollie, who really needed a home....

"Hi, Caitlin! And this is Aidan, right? Your mom called to say you'd be coming. I'm Anna, one of the volunteers. I'm hoping to be a vet, so I help out here on the weekends, and Lucy asked me to show you around. Lucy is the manager, the lady your mom spoke to."

Caitlin nodded and held up her camera. "That's really nice of you. Is it okay if I take some pictures?" she asked nervously.

She'd been looking forward to coming to the rescue center ever since Aidan had agreed to take her, but this morning, she'd suddenly realized it would mean a lot of talking to people she didn't know, which wasn't her favorite thing.

"Sure! Lucy said you're doing a school project?"

"Yes. It's for our school's Community Week. We raise money for a charity by doing bake sales and other fundraisers. And this year, everyone gets to help choose what that is—we all have to make a presentation about a charity that we think the school should help. My aunt said you were trying to raise money to build new pens, right?"

"That's right, for the dogs. We're getting so many that we need more room for them." She sighed. "Actually, we could do with more room period. We only have a small yard to exercise them in, too. So … what would you like to start with? Cats or dogs?"

"Cats," Caitlin said eagerly. She'd never been desperate for a pet of her own, but after seeing Ollie, she was starting to change her mind. He was so cute. And Dad had said they hadn't had a dog or a cat because she had been little, and she wasn't little anymore....

The cat pens were cleverly designed, built so they could be opened up into a little outdoor area, and with shelves for the cats to sleep on. Anna explained that most cats liked being high up because it made them feel safe. They didn't really like to sleep on the floor. Caitlin and Aidan ooohed and ahhhed at all of the kittens— especially a beautiful orange and white pair—but there were so many more fully grown cats. A lot of them had come to the rescue center because their owners had been elderly and had moved into places that couldn't take cats, Anna told them. It was so sad.

30

"Should we go and see the dogs now?"
Anna suggested, and Caitlin jumped
up. She'd been crouching by the last
of the cat pens, trying to coax a sleepy
tabby to come and be petted, but the
cat only yawned and flicked her ears.

"Oh! Yes, please. I already have so
many great pictures for my school
project, though. Are you sure you're
not supposed to be doing something
else?"

Anna smiled. "No, it's okay. I do
whatever needs doing. I'd rather show
you two around than scrub water bowls!"

Caitlin looked back regretfully at
the orange kittens and followed Anna
through a heavy door. She guessed that
the rescue center had to keep the dogs
and cats separated so that they didn't

upset each other.

The dogs' section of the rescue center felt completely different—it was so much noisier! The barking and whining started as soon as the dogs heard the door open, and Caitlin jumped.

"They're loud, aren't they?" Anna grinned at her. "It's hard for them being shut in so much of the time. One of the other jobs I do is take out a couple of dogs at a time to the park around the corner. It makes a big difference if they can get a good walk."

"There are so many…," Caitlin said, looking down the long hallway lined with pens.

"And all of these are full?" Aidan asked.

"Yup." Anna sighed, leading the way

down the hallway as the dogs whined and barked to be noticed. There were dogs pawing eagerly at almost every door. "We have to turn animals away sometimes when we don't have any more room."

Aidan nodded, and then he brightened up, crouching to peer into one of the pens. "Hey, Caitlin, look!"

Caitlin leaned over his shoulder, peering at the dog inside. He was a lot smaller than most of the others—still a puppy, she realized.

"He's really cute, isn't he?" Aidan said, laughing as the little dog scratched eagerly at the wire on his door.

"That's Winston." Anna came over to see who they were looking at. "He's a whippet crossed with we're not sure what. Maybe a Jack Russell—he has a Jack Russell-ish tail. Isn't he beautiful?"

"He's such a pretty color," Caitlin said admiringly. "I've never seen a dog like that before! He's striped!" She crouched down next to Aidan, and the puppy pressed his nose up against the wire door and tried to lick their faces. He was a beautiful, soft blue-gray color, with peach stripes and a white chest and paws. His fur was very smooth, except for the brush-like tail.

"I think the stripes are the whippet in him," Anna explained. "They come in brindle stripes like that often. Do you want to meet him? I can open the pen for you."

"Oh, yes, please!" Caitlin wriggled back so Anna could open the door, and the excited puppy bounced all over her and Aidan, wriggling and licking and whining.

"His fur is almost silky," Caitlin said, running her hand over his smooth back. "It's so short and fine."

"One of the other volunteers is knitting him a sweater." Anna leaned down to pet Winston, too. "Seriously!" she added when Aidan made a face. "He needs one. Whippets get cold easily because they're so skinny and their fur is thin. She's trying to make him one that matches his stripes, a kind of blue-gray camo pattern."

"How old is he?" Caitlin asked. "He looks so little."

"About three months." Anna tickled the puppy under his chin, looking sad. "Someone left him and the rest of the litter outside the police station in a box, and one of the police officers brought them to us."

Caitlin stared at her in shock. "Who would do something like that?"

Anna shrugged. "I don't know. I guess they didn't want puppies. Winston's two sisters went to new homes last week, and he's missing them like crazy. He cries every time someone goes past."

"Ohhh…," Caitlin gulped. She could imagine how sad the beautiful little dog must be, left alone.

The puppy looked up at her and stopped bouncing around. Instead, he gazed at Caitlin with his head to one side and put one small white paw on her knee, as if to tell her that it was all right. *He* was all right.

"You're such a sweetheart," Caitlin whispered. "I can't believe someone dumped you in a box. I came here thinking I might meet a beautiful kitten, but you're even cuter than the cats. I'd take care of you so well if you were mine...."

Chapter Three
An Exciting Time

"Oh, he's adorable!" Caitlin's mom leaned over the table where Caitlin had laid out her photos. "Look at those big brown eyes!"

"I know! And the way his ears fold over. He's my favorite. His name is Winston. I took a bunch of pictures of him. I think I might make him the star of my project. Wouldn't you

want to choose the Garland Animal
Rescue Center as your school charity
if you saw a picture of him? And if you
heard that he'd been abandoned in a
cardboard box?"

"Was he really?" Caitlin's mom
looked shocked. "But he's so sweet!"

"Just wait until he has a sweater
on," Aidan put in, picking up another
photo of Winston. "Caitlin, did you
take photos of any of the other dogs?"

"Yes! I didn't print out as many, that's all.... Mom, can I go to the rescue center again?"

Her mom looked surprised. "But you have plenty of pictures already. You don't need more than this, do you?"

"No.... I didn't mean for the project. But the girl who showed us around, Anna, is a volunteer. She said one of the things she does is take out the dogs for walks in the park. And I was thinking that maybe I could do that."

"That's a nice thought, Caitlin, but I would think you need to be a little older," her mom said, shaking her head.

"I'm almost 10, Mom! It's my birthday in two weeks," Caitlin pointed out.

"Actually, Anna said there are some children who walk the dogs," Aiden said. "But not on their own—they have to go with another volunteer." He picked up a picture of Winston. "I think she said something about getting a form filled out by your parents. Caitlin was probably too busy falling in love with this puppy to notice."

Caitlin squeaked and threw her arms around him. "I didn't hear you talking to her about that! You're so smart!"

Aidan patted her on the head, which usually made Caitlin furious, but she'd forgive him anything right this minute. "Like I said, it was when you were cuddling Winston—you wouldn't have noticed if I'd yelled in your ear! It's okay, Mom; it's not far to Garland Park on a bike, and there's a bike path most of the way. I don't mind going with Caitlin the first time. There were some really cool dogs there, and it'd be fun to walk them. And she could probably go on her own once she knows the way."

He dug a crumpled piece of paper out of his pocket and handed it to their mom. "Forms. Anna gave them to me. I forgot. There you go."

"Can we go tomorrow? Please?"

Caitlin looked pleadingly at her mom. "When I finish my homework?"

Caitlin spent the evening making a huge display board all about the rescue center, with pictures of the dogs and cats, and the small space that the dogs had to run around in. Even if she couldn't convince her class to choose the rescue center as their charity, which she guessed wasn't all that likely, she definitely wanted to do something to help.

The picture in the middle of the board was of Winston, the one her mom had liked where his eyes were so big, and he looked so sad and cute.

After all the time she'd spent looking at pictures of the little whippet, Caitlin couldn't wait to see him again for real. She even took Aidan a bacon sandwich in bed on Sunday morning to try and persuade him that it was time to get up. But he ate the sandwich in about three bites, handed her back the plate, and pulled the comforter over his head.

It was more than an hour later that her brother finally surfaced, and he insisted on eating a second breakfast before they left. Caitlin couldn't eat. She was too excited. She sat there watching every mouthful of toast until Aidan groaned and finally gave up.

"I can't eat with you staring at me like that," he muttered. "Come on. I'll text Dad and tell him we're going now and we'll be back for lunch, okay? Go and get your bike."

Caitlin didn't think she'd ever ridden so fast, and Aidan was right—the rescue center wasn't far. She could definitely do the ride on her own if Mom and Dad would let her.

She hurried into the rescue center, clutching the forms worriedly. What if they said she was too young? It would be awful. But Anna was there, and she laughed.

"Look, Lucy—I told you she'd be back!"

"We have the forms you gave Aidan," Caitlin said, her voice not much more than a whisper. She held them out to Lucy. "Um. Is it okay if we help out a little? Can we walk the dogs?"

Aidan came in from locking up the bikes, and Lucy smiled at them both. "Of course you can." She scanned the form. "Yes, we have all of your contact numbers, and this looks fine. There are a few health and safety rules we need to explain before we can let you go out, though. For starters, you'll only be able to walk the smaller dogs, Caitlin—a lot of our dogs aren't used to walking nicely on a leash, so it can be hard work. But we'll send you out with an adult volunteer, too."

Caitlin nodded. She kind of expected that—they weren't going to let her take a huge Labrador to the park on her own.

"And sometimes we need people to stay here, too," Lucy added. "Even playing with the dogs in the yard can be really helpful."

"We don't mind what we do, do we?" Aidan said, looking at Caitlin. "And we can help with the cats, too—Anna said you need people to groom them."

"Yes, and to spend time with the younger ones," Lucy agreed. "Okay! I'll tell you what, Anna—why don't you take Aidan and Caitlin and a few of the younger dogs out into the yard for a little while first? The official name for this is socialization," she added, "but it basically means showing them how to have fun."

Caitlin nodded eagerly. It sounded like the best possible job to her— spending the morning playing with dogs. She wasn't quite brave enough to ask if Winston was going to be one of the younger dogs that Lucy meant. After all, she wasn't volunteering only for him....

There was a door opening. Winston bounced up hopefully, his thin tail whipping from side to side. Were they coming for him? Could he go out? He scratched hopefully at the wire, standing up on his hind legs and whining.

No. They were walking past him. Winston dropped down onto all four paws and stood watching mournfully as they went on down the hallway and started to open up other doors. They were putting leashes on the dogs. So they were going out.

Winston's tail drooped as he slunk back to his cushion and slumped down with his chin on his paws.

Then one of his flopped-over ears twitched, and he peered sideways from his cushion. Was that someone coming back? There were footsteps coming closer. He tensed up, ready to spring to the door, hoping they wouldn't just go past again....

The door of his pen rattled, and he bounced up, whimpering with excitement. Yes! His door was opening! Winston whirled around the pen, barking and yipping and dancing in circles. A walk—he was actually getting to go outside!

He kind of knew that he needed to hold still long enough for them to clip the leash onto his collar, but he was too excited. He kept on barking and dancing until eventually, the smaller girl knelt down and caught him so the older one could put his leash on. He nuzzled at the smaller girl, licking her cheek and feeling her laugh. He wriggled so much that he scrambled himself into her lap and felt her arms go around him, warm and tight.

Chapter Four
Helping Out

Caitlin giggled as Winston danced around her feet, bouncing excitedly on the end of his leash.

"How do you ever get him to walk anywhere?" Aidan asked Anna. He was holding on to a small brown terrier named Billy, and Billy was watching Winston with his ears flattened back as if he were horrified.

"He's better when he gets outside and there's stuff to look at and sniff. Actually, once he's fully grown, he'll probably be able to run really fast. Whippets are great runners—they're like greyhounds, but smaller."

"I looked them up," Caitlin admitted. "One of the websites said that if you let them off the leash, they can disappear, and you have no hope of catching them."

"Exactly. Winston might not be as bad, because he's only half whippet, but we'd still say to his new owners that he's best kept on a leash until he's really well trained. Okay, here's the play area. We can let them off the leash in here because it's all closed in, but we have to watch to make sure they're getting along okay."

Anna pulled open a door that led to

a small fenced area of scruffy grass, scattered with chewed rubber balls and rope toys. Then she crouched down and unhooked the leash on Pickle, the fluffy white Westie she'd brought out.

The two older dogs nosed cautiously onto the grass, but Winston bounced past them as soon as Caitlin unhooked his leash. He shot across the yard, ignoring the toys that Billy and Pickle started to nose at, and leaped around wildly.

"He really does love being outside!" Caitlin said to Anna, watching him bound around.

"He could do with a bigger space, to be honest," Anna said. "He's only a puppy, but see how strong his back legs are already?"

Caitlin nodded and then giggled
as Winston came racing back toward
them. He looked like he was running
straight for her and Anna, as though
he were going to crash right into them,
but at the last second he swerved aside,
jumping up to lick at Caitlin's arm.

"He's so funny!" Anna shook her
head. "He seems to really like you too.
Maybe if you came after school one

56

day this week, Lucy would let you take
him out to the park. He could have
more of a run then. He doesn't need
that much exercise now because he's so
little, but he loved it when I took him
there the other day."

Caitlin nodded, her eyes shining.
Anna thought that Winston liked
her! She watched as he dashed over
to the other end of the yard and then
she crouched down, patting her knees
hopefully. Would he understand what

she meant? Would he even want to
come?

But the little brindle dog came
hurtling back down the yard and flung
himself at her, making excited *roo,
roo* noises that Caitlin had never
heard from any dog before.

"Yes, you're beautiful,
aren't you?" she said,
giggling as he licked
her ears and then
jumped down
to wriggle on his
back on the grass,
waving his paws
in the air and
still singing
with happiness.

Aidan came to stand next to her,

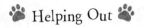
shaking his head. "Caitlin, what did you *do* to that dog?"

Caitlin's mom dropped her off at the rescue center on Tuesday afternoon— she'd wanted to go on Monday, but she had a swimming lesson. Caitlin had been hoping to walk Winston, but she didn't feel brave enough to ask Lucy. She'd do it next time, she promised herself. Instead, she got to take Pickle out to the park with Christine, one of the older volunteers. She did say hello to Winston on the way to find Pickle, though.

"I've been coming here to help out for years," Christine explained. "I live in an apartment where I can't have my own dog, so I love getting the chance to spend time with the dogs at the rescue center."

"Don't you miss them?" Caitlin asked her after a while. "When they get adopted, I mean?" She'd been a little shy about talking to Christine at first, but then the big husky that Christine was walking had looped his leash around Christine's feet and tripped her up. By the time Caitlin had hauled her up again and helped brush the mud off her coat, a lot of the shyness was gone.

"Of course. But then you have to think of the homes they've gone to and how happy they are now. People send us pictures sometimes, too, which is always nice." Christine looked at her, smiling. "I know which one you're thinking of. That little whippet mix. Winston. He's

beautiful, isn't he?"

Caitlin stared at her in surprise.

"You spent a good 10 minutes talking to him through his pen door when you first arrived! I'll tell you what—how about we take these two back—I think Pickle has had enough anyway—and see if Lucy thinks Winston would like to go out for a run. I bet Millie would love a walk, too; she's the Labrador mix in the pen by the door."

Walking Winston was even more fun than playing with him in the yard. Caitlin hadn't realized how fast he could be. She had to run, too, since she couldn't let him off the leash, and she chased after him, panting and laughing. Luckily, Winston ran about three times as far as she did, dashing backward and forward.

"Maybe he needs one of those extending leashes," Christine said when she caught up with them and saw Caitlin panting, with her hands on her knees, and Winston looking up at her impatiently.

"No!" Caitlin squeaked. Then her cheeks turned pink. "I'm sorry.... It's just.... I read about those on a dog website. They're dangerous for whippets because they go so fast. If they pull the leash all the way out and then it stops them suddenly, it can hurt their necks really badly. They're supposed to have a long leash that you hold in loops. Or if you really want to use an extending leash, you need to use it with a harness, not a collar. One that goes around his middle." Caitlin held her hands around Winston's tiny shoulders, trying to show Christine what she meant, and Christine grinned at her.

"I didn't know that. You've been doing a lot of research."

Caitlin's cheeks turned even pinker. "I had to for my school project," she explained.

"Not because you've fallen in love with a whippet?"

"Maybe a little." Caitlin sighed. After

swimming last night, she'd spent a long time on her mom's laptop, looking up whippets. It seemed like the funny noises Winston made were a whippet thing—there were even videos online of whippet owners getting their dogs to "sing" on command. And so many pictures of whippets on couches and whippets sneaking onto people's beds!

Caitlin could imagine Winston climbing onto her bed and getting under the comforter. Whippets had to have blankets to snuggle in; a lot of the websites said so. It was because they were so skinny, it was hard for them to keep warm. Even though Winston was only half whippet, he was definitely a skinny little thing.

"So when do you have to speak to

everyone at school about the rescue center?" Christine asked. "You sounded a little nervous about it when you were telling me earlier."

"Next Monday." Caitlin gave a little shudder. "My friend Lily is really excited about it—she's like that. She loves standing up in front of everyone, but I hate it." She shook herself determinedly. "I don't care, though. I'm still going to do it. If my class chooses the rescue center, it'll go on a list of seven for the principal and the teachers to pick from. One idea from each class. And the school does all kinds of stuff for the charity they choose—sponsored sleepovers and a car wash … and bake sales. Last year, we raised almost one thousand dollars! Wouldn't that buy at

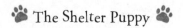

least part of a new dog area?"

Christine nodded. "Of course it would. It would be great to have some extra money coming in. But even what you've done this afternoon is a big help, you know. Pickle and Winston wouldn't have gotten a walk today if you hadn't come to the rescue center."

"I guess so." Caitlin reached down to rub Winston's silky whippet ears. "But maybe me and my friends could try to raise some money, too. I just wish there was something more that I could do."

Winston sat on the grass with his eyes closed and his nose pointing to the sky. He loved having his ears rubbed.

66

Caitlin was pulling them gently
through her fingers now, and she was
giggling. She seemed happy, too. It
was sunny and warm, and he'd raced
all over the park with her—he'd run so
fast that he was feeling very worn out
and relaxed now, especially with all the
fussing over his ears. Winston slumped
down, his nose
resting
on his
paws, and
groaned with
sleepy happiness.

"He's purring!" Caitlin whispered.
"I didn't know dogs could purr!"

"Neither did I," said Christine,
laughing. "But it definitely sounds like
it."

Winston rolled over onto his back, waving his little white paws in the air, still purring.

"We've got to go back, Winston," Caitlin called gently. "Time to go home. Christine, I think he's asleep! We must have walked him for too long."

"Well, he is only a puppy."

Winston hardly noticed when Caitlin picked him up. His eyelids flickered a little, and then he snuggled closer in to her shirt. His sleepy purr deepened to a little whippet snore.

Caitlin jumped carefully down from the branch of the big tree in the yard and looked up at the banner.

"It's a little lopsided," Sean said, squinting at it, but Lily glared at him.

"It's perfect, Caitlin," she said. "Don't go back up in the tree. It's too wobbly. I kept thinking you were going to fall. And it doesn't matter if it's lopsided. Everyone can see what it says."

Caitlin made a face. "At least you can read it. I had to squash up the words 'rescue center' because I was running out of space. Oh, well."

"Can I buy this?" Alice asked hopefully, holding up a Barbie doll from one of the bags Lily had piled on the table.

"Do you have any money?" Caitlin asked, surprised.

"No.... But only because Mom ran out of change so she couldn't give us our allowance. I'll pay later," Alice promised.

"My mom thinks this is a great idea," Lily told Caitlin. "I finally cleaned out my closet. And look what she sent." She fished around in another one of her bags and opened up a big box of brownies. "She said we can eat them or sell them. She doesn't mind."

"Sell them!" Caitlin said, at the same time as Alice and Sean said, "Eat them!"

"Oh, okay. You can each have one, but we'll sell the rest," Caitlin allowed.

She walked around the front of the table, looking at it admiringly. They'd put more printouts of the pictures she'd taken along the front, and a description of the new space the rescue center wanted to build for the dogs—she'd found that on the website. Mom had helped her make a batch of sugar cookies, and Aunt Jen had sent chocolate cupcakes with Alice and Sean.

Now all they needed were customers. The problem was, Caitlin's street wasn't very busy. An hour later, Alice was sulking because Caitlin wouldn't let her eat any more cupcakes, and Sean had decided that most of the old toys he'd brought to sell he wanted to keep after all. They'd sold some brownies to Mrs. Marsh, who lived next door, but that was about it.

"How's it going?" Caitlin's mom

came out onto the front step.

Caitlin sighed and slumped down on the grass. "No one is coming by. We made all the cupcakes and everything, but we don't have any customers."

"Oh, honey. I'm sorry. But I'm sure it'll get better."

Ten minutes later, Caitlin was starting to feel like giving up when Lily came running back down the street. She'd taken some brownies to see if she could sell them to one of her friends who lived on the next street. "Caitlin! Your brother is coming, with a whole bunch of people!"

Caitlin got up off the grass and ran to look where Lily was pointing.

"Where's he been?" Lily asked. "Who are they?"

"He went out to play soccer. That's everyone from his team!" Caitlin dashed back to stand behind the table. "And the team they were playing, too, by the looks of it. Mom must have called him! Put out all the cupcakes! Make it look nice!"

Caitlin didn't think the soccer team would want her old toys, or Lily's, but maybe some of them had little sisters. By the time they left, there wasn't a crumb of cupcake left, and most of the toys had been sold, too.

"We made forty dollars!" Lily yelped, tipping the coins back into the ice-cream tub that they'd been keeping the sales money in.

Caitlin hugged her and then hugged Aidan. "Thank you, thank you, thank you! I'm going to the rescue center this afternoon—I can give them the money then."

Chapter Five
A Little Sadness

Miss Lewis beamed at Lily and wrote the name of the riding school on the whiteboard. "Nice job, Lily. That was a great idea. Okay.... Caitlin, you're next."

Caitlin knew she was—they were going around table by table, so she had to be. She'd sat through Lily's talk with her heart thumping so hard that it seemed to be blocking her throat, and her hands were icy cold.

She wasn't entirely sure how she got to the front of the classroom, but she was there, and everyone was staring at her. Caitlin stared back for what seemed like forever and then forced herself to look at the picture of Winston in the middle of her poster board. He was 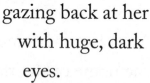 gazing back at her with huge, dark eyes.

Caitlin took a deep breath. "My charity is the Garland Animal Rescue Center. It's near here,

over by Garland Park. They take in
a lot of dogs and cats every month,
and they always need more money.
This is Winston...." She pointed to
his picture. "He's only three months
old—or about that. No one knows
exactly because he was dumped
outside the police station in a
cardboard box...." She heard the gasp
as she said it, and everyone leaned
forward to look at the picture, and
then Miss Lewis had to tell the class
to shush.

After that, the talk felt a lot easier,
and Caitlin was almost surprised
when she got to the end. It seemed
to have gone a lot faster than when
she had practiced it with Dad. And
everyone clapped!

"That was great, Caitlin! What a beautiful dog. And cute kittens, too. Okay, just a couple more presentations, and then it's time for the voting. Lakshmi, it's your turn next."

"Great job!" Lily whispered. "I thought you said you were really nervous, but you didn't sound it at all."

"I was!" Caitlin smiled at her in relief. "I had to keep looking at Winston to make me talk."

Lily sighed. "I'll have to come to the rescue center and see him. He's so sweet."

There were 27 different charities up on the board by the end of the morning. Miss Lewis said that they would do the actual voting after lunch once they'd all had a chance to think about it.

"I'll vote for the rescue center," Lily promised as she opened her lunch box. "I might have even if we *were* allowed to vote for our own charity. I can't believe someone left those puppies in a box."

"I will, too." James leaned across the table. "And I'm going to get my mom and dad to look at the website. I've been asking them if we can have a dog forever, and they've kind of said yes. That puppy is so cute; he'd definitely persuade my mom. And I bet my dad would love him, too."

Caitlin stared at him and tried to smile. Of course, she wanted everyone in the class to vote for the rescue center. And of course, she wanted Winston to have a new home. But

… not just yet. She and Christine were going to try to train Winston to walk to heel. She'd even found a pattern for a whippet scarf, and she'd been planning to get Mom to help her knit one. There wouldn't be time if Winston found a new home so quickly—she needed him to stay at the rescue center a little longer....

Caitlin swallowed hard. In fact, she didn't want Winston to go to a new owner at all.

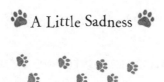

A Little Sadness

"That's amazing, Caitlin." Lucy gave her a hug. "You should be really proud of yourself." She looked down at Caitlin and tipped her head to one side. "For someone who's just gotten the whole school to choose her favorite charity to support, you don't look very happy."

Caitlin looked down at her feet. "Everyone thought Winston was really cute when I showed them the pictures yesterday," she explained. "James in my class has been trying to persuade his parents to get a dog. And he said that he was going to show them Winston on the website. Then he came running up to me on the playground this morning, and he said his mom is going to call you today about coming to see Winston. Sometime this weekend, probably."

"Ohhh.... I see." Lucy hugged her again. "It's the hardest thing about volunteering here. Why do you think I have four cats at home?"

"Four?" Caitlin laughed and sniffed at the same time.

"Yup. I couldn't resist.... I'd have dogs, too, except that I'm not home enough. And the cats would never forgive me."

Caitlin nodded. "My mom and dad both work. Not always at the same time, though. I'd started thinking that maybe we *could* have a dog. A little dog, because our house isn't very big. And me and my brother could do the walking. I was working my way up to talking to them about it, but I was worried that they'd say no. We've always had small pets—my dad has fish, and my brother has gerbils and a rat." She sniffed again. "Now it's too late."

"I promise there'll be another dog that you fall in love with," Lucy said gently. "And think how happy Winston will be with someone to give him all of the attention he wants."

Caitlin nodded. Of course, she wanted someone to make Winston happy. But she wanted that person to be *her*.

"Are you going to be here this weekend?" Lucy asked her. "I'm thinking about who's going to be around when, for exercising the dogs. Anna's here, but Christine is away."

"Mom says I can come on Saturday. Not Sunday, though, because it's my birthday."

"Oh, nice. Are you having a party?"

Caitlin shook her head. "I don't know. Mom is arranging it. My friend Lily is coming over, and we're going somewhere special, but it's a surprise. Last year, we went to the beach, and it was so much fun. But Mom says the weather forecast isn't that good for this weekend."

And somehow, she just couldn't get excited about whatever it was that they were going to do. She'd almost rather be at the rescue center, spending precious time with Winston before he was adopted. James and his family wouldn't be able to take Winston home with them, even if they came on Saturday—not until Lucy or one of the other staff had gone to do a home check. She had just a little bit longer to wish he was hers.

Winston dashed down to the end of
the yard, chasing after the ball. He
shook it fiercely for a minute and then
dropped it and hurried back to Caitlin.

"You're supposed to bring it to *me*,
silly." She rubbed his ears gently, and
Winston leaned against her. Caitlin
wasn't running up and down with him
and laughing, like she usually
did. She was sitting on
the grass instead, with
one arm wrapped
around her
knees, and she
kept petting
him, over
and over.

That was nice—he liked being petted. But something seemed different. He rested his nose on her knee and stared up at her worriedly. Something wasn't right. *She* wasn't right.

"What's the matter, Winston? Look, here's another ball." Caitlin threw it down to the end of the yard, but Winston didn't chase after it. Instead, he came around to the side of her and climbed determinedly into her lap, snuggling himself half inside her hoodie. She was warm, but that wasn't why. He wanted to be next to her.

She needed him.

Chapter Six
The Visit

"Is that your friend from school?" Lucy whispered to Caitlin as James and his family came up the front steps.

"Yes." Caitlin swallowed.

"Do you want to go and help with the cats?" Lucy suggested gently. "I know how you feel about Winston. You don't have to be around if it's going to make you sad."

Caitlin shook her head. "James knows I'm going to be here. It would be weird if I didn't say hello."

"And Winston likes you," Lucy pointed out. "He'll probably be a little less shy if you're around, too. Hello! You're the Logans? You've come to look at Winston?"

Caitlin recognized James's mom from the school playground, and his younger sister was in the grade below them at school. "Hi, James. Hi, Abbie."

"Caitlin volunteers at the rescue center," Lucy explained.

"Yes, and it was Caitlin who showed James the picture of Winston," James's dad said, smiling at her. "He looks like the perfect dog for us, Caitlin. Thank you!"

Caitlin smiled at him, even though she didn't feel like it. She thought her smile probably looked a little fake, but no one seemed to notice.

"Should I get Winston out of his pen and bring him into the yard?" she suggested to Lucy. If people asked to look at a particular dog, they got to spend some time with him or her in the yard or a little playroom indoors, just to make sure that they all got along.

Caitlin hurried to the pens and

opened Winston's door. Even though she was feeling miserable, she still couldn't help laughing as he danced around her while she tried to put on his leash. She loved it that he was so excited.

"You're going to meet some really nice people," she whispered as she finally managed to clip the leash on to his collar. "They might even take you home. I bet James would love it if you wanted to sleep on his bed. And they'll take you for so many walks. It's going to be wonderful. You might just have to learn to be nice to his cat, that's all," she added, remembering James talking about his cat and the guide dog puppies next door.

Caitlin led Winston out to the yard, where James and his family were waiting with Lucy.

"Oh, he's even cuter than his pictures!" Abbie squeaked, and Caitlin felt Winston press himself against her leg nervously.

"It's okay," she told him. "Come on. Come and see." She coaxed Winston forward, and he peered around her legs at the family, wagging his tail slowly.

"Aren't you beautiful!" James's dad said quietly, crouching down. "Gently, Abbie. Let him get used to us first."

"I read that whippets are touch-sensitive," James's mom said to Lucy, sounding a little worried. "Do we need to be careful petting him? We don't want to scare him."

Caitlin bit her bottom lip. James and Abbie were being so quiet and patient, and James's mom and dad sounded like they were going to be great dog owners. They'd been doing their research, just like she had. She'd been secretly hoping that James and his family would turn out not to be the right home for Winston, but they were perfect.

"As long as you're careful and he can see what you're doing, he won't get startled. Do you want to take his leash?" Lucy suggested to James's dad, and Caitlin handed it over.

"I'll go and … and…." She didn't really know what she was going to do. Caitlin ducked back through the door into the main dog area. She just couldn't watch anymore.

The Visit

Winston turned to look as Caitlin slipped out of the door and pulled a little on his leash to follow her. There were other people around him now, and he couldn't see where Caitlin went. He whined worriedly, not sure what was going on, but Lucy was there, whispering gently to him and rubbing his ears.

He liked Lucy. She brought his food most days, and she always stopped to pet him and talk to him. The people with her were talking to him and petting him, too. Maybe it was all right that Caitlin wasn't there, but he wished she'd stayed. He liked the way she rubbed his ears best and the way she whispered to him. He was sure that Caitlin hadn't gone far. Maybe she was just beyond that door....

"Winston?" Lucy was calling to him, and he turned, letting her show him a ball so the children could throw it for him to chase. A run up and down the yard! That was what he wanted.

But it would have been better if Caitlin had stayed.

Caitlin leaned against the wall just inside the yard door. It wasn't completely shut, and she could hear Abbie and James laughing and talking to Winston. It sounded like he was totally failing to fetch a ball again. He

just wasn't very good at it. He loved
the racing around, though.

She probably should go back out
there and smile and be nice and tell
James's family how handsome Winston
was. As if they couldn't see that for
themselves already. Or she should do
what Lucy had suggested and go and
help Anna feed the cats. Anything
except stand here listening to the family
falling in love with her adorable puppy.
But she couldn't drag herself away.

Caitlin blinked, realizing that there
was a change in the voices outside.
They were quieter, more worried.
Uncertainly, she moved closer to the
door, wondering what was going on.

"And is he a fairly young cat?" Lucy
was asking.

"Yes, that's my only worry about getting a dog," James's mom said. "Biscuit is a little nervous. I don't want to upset him. That's one reason we wanted to get a puppy. We thought an older dog might find it harder to accept living with a cat—but a puppy wouldn't know any different."

Lucy was silent for a minute, and Caitlin peeked around the door to see her. She was looking worried.

"Usually, I'd absolutely agree with you. Puppies do learn to live with cats, and it's not a problem for most dogs...."

"What's the matter?" James asked. "Doesn't Winston like cats?"

"To be honest, he's never really met one," Lucy said, smiling at him. "But it's his breed that's the problem. He's half whippet, and whippets are what are called sighthounds. That means that they were bred to be hunting dogs, and they hunted by sight, not smell. Winston is going to have whippet instincts. That means he's going to want to chase anything small and furry that's running away from him."

"Oh...." James's dad made a face. "That sounds like Biscuit...."

"I'm not saying that he would." Lucy

frowned a little. "Just that he *might*. It's a risk. And for that reason, we'd never recommend adopting a sighthound where there's already a cat in the family."

Caitlin turned back from the door and pressed her hand over her mouth. She was smiling an enormous smile, and she knew she shouldn't be, but she couldn't help it....

Chapter Seven
Time with Winston

"James's family is going to take Millie home instead," Caitlin told Winston as she filled up his food bowl. "Her old owner had a cat, and she was really good and didn't chase him or anything like that. Lucy thinks she might miss him, actually." She watched Winston gobble down his food. "I bet you'd have loved living with James and Abbie.

They're nice. They'd have made such a big fuss of you. I wonder if you really would have chased their cat." It was hard to imagine Winston being so fierce—he was such a sweet, friendly puppy. But Lucy had explained to her afterward that it wasn't something he would decide to do—it was a hunting instinct, and it had been part of whippets for centuries.

"Even if you're not going to be James's dog, you're going to get a new owner soon...." Caitlin crouched down, watching Winston wolf down his dog biscuits. "You're too beautiful to stay here for long—your sisters didn't, did they? And everyone in my class thought you were adorable." She sighed. "I have to get used to it. Lucy says I'll fall in love with another dog once you're gone...."

Winston glanced up from his bowl of food and stared at her. He looked as if he was outraged by the idea, and Caitlin giggled. "No, I don't think so, either. But someone's going to want to take you home any day now." She shivered. "It could even be tomorrow. Unless I persuade Mom and Dad that we should adopt you instead. And to be honest, I can't see that working. Even though they do keep saying how great it is that I'm helping at the rescue center, I don't think they really want a dog."

Caitlin sat down on the floor, leaning against the wall of the pen. "I probably should go and help feed all of the others. Lucy hasn't said it, but it isn't fair if I keep making a big fuss over you. I've got to let you fall in love with a new owner." She rubbed the back of her arm across her eyes. "I just can't help thinking that you'd be so much better off with me...."

Winston licked the last pieces of dog biscuit out of his bowl and stared at it hopefully, just in case any more food suddenly arrived, but it didn't. He padded over to Caitlin and rested his nose on her knee.

"Maybe I should get Mom and Dad to come and visit. Then maybe they'd want to take you home," Caitlin suggested, looking back into his soft, dark eyes. "I don't see how anyone wouldn't want to. Unless they had a cat. And I guess we'd have to be super-careful with Aidan's gerbils, and Trevor. But he keeps them in his room all the time, anyway."

Caitlin ran her hand over Winston's smooth neck, and her voice wobbled. "I can't stand thinking about you going somewhere else and forgetting all about me. Anna said this morning that you always look disappointed when she takes you out to the yard for exercise and I'm not there. I don't know if she was just being nice, but

I do think you're happy to see me, aren't you?"

Winston leaned over to lick her hand, and then he slumped down on the floor of the pen on his back, waving his legs in the air for Caitlin to rub his tummy.

"I can see your dinner! You go skinny little whippet, great big bulge, skinny little whippet."

Winston rolled over again and climbed into Caitlin's lap, snuggling up with a huge, happy sigh. Caitlin sat watching him as he wriggled himself comfy and closed his eyes, and then she petted him, over and over, loving his peach stripes. She was trying to fix them in her mind, she realized, in case he was gone by the time she came back.

"Caitlin!"

"That's Mom," Caitlin whispered, trying to stand up without waking the puppy on her lap. "She said she'd come and pick me up. I'll see you on Tuesday." She swallowed hard. "At least … I hope I will."

Winston curled himself into a ball on Caitlin's lap. He was deliciously full and deliciously warm, and she was petting him. He snoozed, making little whippet whining noises as he dreamed of running through the park and chasing squirrels.

He half woke as she stood up and gently laid him on his cushion. She even pulled a blanket up around him and tucked him in so that he was cozy. But then the metal door of the pen clanged behind her, and Winston woke up.

Caitlin was leaving! She was leaving him behind! He wanted her to stay, to snuggle up with him. Whimpering, he tried to wriggle his way out of the blanket, but it all got tangled around his paws. By the time he'd dragged himself up and across the pen, she was gone. Winston sat down by his door, lifted his head, and wailed.

"Are you okay, Caitlin?" her mom asked as they drove home. "You're so quiet. Usually you come home from the rescue center telling me stories about all of the things the dogs have done, or how you almost lost a guinea pig behind a cupboard, or something...."

Caitlin leaned her head against the car window. "I'm just a little tired."

"So Lucy said that James's family can't take Winston after all? That's sad."

"Yes," Caitlin agreed, even though she didn't think it was. "But she says she's sure someone will adopt him soon."

"You should have taken me to

see him," her mom said, glancing sideways. "We weren't in a hurry. I'd love to meet him now that you've told me so much about him."

"Mom, have you ever wanted to have a dog?" Caitlin asked suddenly.

"Ummm." Her mom was silent for a minute, looking at the street. "We've always been busy just with you and Aidan. It isn't that I *don't* want a dog, I've just never felt desperate to have one. Do you know what I mean?"

"Yes...." Caitlin sighed. It wasn't enough. Her mom and dad would have to pay for food and vet bills and special fleecy harnesses that didn't rub a whippet's skin. They'd have to take Winston for walks and arrange for him to be taken care of when they went on vacation. And everyone in her family needed to be enthusiastic about getting a dog. Caitlin turned back to the window so her mom couldn't see the tears spilling down her cheeks.

Chapter Eight
The Best Birthday Present

Usually Caitlin woke up on her birthday feeling excited. Last year, when she couldn't think of what kind of party she'd like to have, her dad had organized a surprise trip for the four of them and Lily. Caitlin had woken up at six, desperate to find out where they were going. She'd loved it so much that she'd asked for another surprise this year.

But today, she couldn't feel happy. She wasn't looking forward to the trip at all. Would it be really ungrateful to say she didn't want a birthday surprise, and that she'd rather go to the rescue center?

Caitlin sighed and pulled her comforter up over her head. Of course it would. Mom and Dad had planned whatever it was, and they'd arranged for Lily to come over. She couldn't get out of it, no matter much she wanted to. She wondered vaguely what they had planned. Mom was right—it definitely wasn't good enough weather for a beach trip, like last year. That had been such a perfect day—they'd gone swimming and splashed in the ocean, and built sandcastles, and buried her dad in the sand.

Of course, it would have been even

better if they'd had a dog. Did Winston like to dig? Caitlin wondered. She could just imagine him spraying sand everywhere and sneezing as he got it all up his nose. He probably wouldn't want to swim, though, because it would be too cold for him. And one of the websites she'd read said that swimming was harder for whippets because they were so slim, and they didn't have any fat to help them float. But maybe he'd like to paddle....

"Are you are awake under there?"

Caitlin peeked out from under her comforter to see her mom looking around the door. "Mmm...."

"Happy birthday, sweetheart. Are you coming to have breakfast? I have those waffles you really like."

Caitlin nodded. She knew she should be leaping out of bed and racing downstairs, but she didn't feel bouncy and birthday-ish at all. "I'll be down in a minute," she told her mom.

Mom and Dad and Aidan were all sitting at the kitchen table, which was heaped with a pile of birthday cards and presents. And even though Caitlin wasn't in a birthday mood, the presents did look very exciting.

"Now, these are from Grandma, and Nana, and Grandpa," her mom explained. "And there are a couple of little ones from us. But you'll have to wait until later for the rest of your presents."

Caitlin blinked at her, confused. "Why?"

"You'll see what I mean, I promise." Her mom smiled.

"Okay...." Caitlin nodded and started to open the stack of cards. There wasn't a present from Aunt Jen and Alice and Sam, which was odd. They always sent something. Maybe they were coming over to give it to her instead.

"Oh, Lily's here." Caitlin's dad jumped up as the doorbell rang, and Caitlin heard him talking to Lily's mom in the hallway. Lily came dashing into the kitchen and gave her a hug.

"Hello! Happy birthday! Did you get any good presents? I've got you one, but you can't open it now—you have to wait until later."

Caitlin turned to look accusingly at her mom and her dad, who'd followed Lily back into the kitchen.

"Do my presents have something to

do with my birthday trip?" she asked. "Where are we going? This is really weird...."

"Don't worry. It's worth the wait." Aidan stuffed half a waffle in his mouth and then talked through it. "You're going to love it. Promise."

Caitlin passed the plate of waffles to Lily and nibbled on the edge of hers—they were her favorite breakfast food, but today she wasn't feeling all that hungry. And even though she was still feeling sad about Winston, she couldn't help being curious about where they were going. Everyone else seemed so excited. Lily wouldn't stop giggling to herself, and her mom and dad kept giving each other conspiratorial looks.

"You have to tell me what's going

on!" she burst out.

"Not a chance," her dad said, grinning. "But it is time to go. Aidan, do you have the blindfold?"

"A blindfold?" Caitlin squeaked. "Why?"

Aidan made a *duh!* noise. "So you can't see where we're going!"

"You can't be mean to her. It's her birthday," Lily said sternly. "Put it on, Caitlin. We want to go!"

"Okay…," Caitlin muttered. "This is so strange." But she stood up and let Aidan wrap one of her mom's scarves over her eyes.

"How many fingers am I holding up?"

"I don't *know!*"

"All right. She can't see. Lily, you take her other arm. Come on, Caitlin."

Caitlin felt them grab her arms, and she stumbled down the hallway and out of the front of the house. Someone unlocked the car—she heard it beep. "So we're going in the car?" she asked. She wasn't sure if she was excited or nervous, but her stomach was doing somersaults.

"Don't bang your head on the door," Lily said. "Duck down a little. This is so funny, Caitlin. It's the best birthday surprise ever, I promise."

"Are we going a long way?" Caitlin asked as she fumbled with her seat belt. She was in the middle, between Lily and Aidan.

"Ummm…," Lily sounded doubtful.

"No more questions," Caitlin's mom said firmly. "We don't want you guessing. It has to be a surprise."

Caitlin leaned back against the car seat, biting her bottom lip. It felt so weird, driving without being able to see where they were going. She was almost shocked when the car stopped a few minutes later, and she could hear Aidan and Lily unhooking their seat belts. "Are we here?" she asked, turning her head from side to side, trying to figure out where they might be. They'd gone about as far as her school, she figured, but that didn't make sense.

"Yup. Here, come this way." Aidan

pulled her gently, and Caitlin climbed out of the car and stood waiting. There weren't any clues to where she was— the only sounds were cars going by. They could be anywhere.

"Up the steps," her dad said, and she felt his arm around her shoulders, leading her forward. Someone opened a door—Caitlin could hear its squeaky *whoosh* noise—and then she knew where they were.

She could smell it. The special disinfectant they used to clean up— and now that she'd figured it out, she could hear barking, too, very quiet barking, muffled by the doors to the dog pens.

They were at the rescue center.

Caitlin turned, grabbing at her dad's

arm. "Dad? What are we doing here?"

Lucy laughed—Caitlin was sure it was her. She guessed Lucy must be standing behind the reception desk. "I told you she'd know as soon as she arrived!"

"Awww, I was hoping we'd get you as far as the pen," Caitlin's mom said. "You can take the blindfold off now, sweetheart."

Caitlin reached up to pull it off and looked around at them all. Everyone was beaming at her, but she couldn't see why. Or why they'd brought her here.

"You still haven't figured it out, have you?" said Aidan with a huge grin.

"No...."

"We were going to take you and Lily ice skating," her mom explained. "But then we changed our minds. Look." She nodded toward the door that led to the dog pens, and Anna, who was pushing it open with her shoulder. Her hands were full with a small, blue-gray striped dog, a dog who had started to make silly, happy, yipping noises as soon as he saw Caitlin.

"Now, just keep in mind that Winston is absolutely not your birthday present, as it's not a good idea to give pets as presents, and he's going to belong to the whole family…," Dad explained.

"But his collar and leash and the basket and blankets and bowls and toys and the huge book about whippets Dad found—all of that *is* your birthday present," Aidan put in.

"And I bought you an awesome T-shirt with a whippet on it," Lily said. "Me and Mom found it yesterday. I wanted you to be wearing it when you got him, but I thought you might guess. And if you didn't guess, it would make you miserable again."

"Miserable?" Caitlin asked, blinking as Anna gently put Winston into her arms and he wriggled, trying to lick her all over.

"You've been miserable all week, Caitlin! Even when Mr. Turner was telling everyone in the assembly that the school was going to support the rescue center and help build new pens for more dogs, you looked so sad! It's been ever since James said he wanted to adopt Winston. I told your mom on the playground when you forgot your notebook on Wednesday."

Caitlin turned around to stare at her mom over Winston's head.

"We'd already been so impressed by everything you were doing, Caitlin. You were working so hard, coming here after school, and then doing your yard sale. Aidan said you were desperate for a dog. I called the rescue center to ask if someone could do a home check for us that weekend. And then Lily told me how much you loved Winston—but when I spoke to Lucy, James's family had already arranged to come and see him. I couldn't believe I was too late."

"I called your mom as soon as we realized they wouldn't be able to take Winston because of their cat," Lucy told her, smiling. "She and your dad came in to see him last night."

"When we left you with Aidan because we said we had a couple of special last-minute birthday things to get," her dad explained, "we were here. And then we went to the big pet store outside town."

"But … but I didn't think you

wanted a dog! Mom, you said, in the car yesterday!"

"Yes, well, I couldn't exactly say, yes I'd love a dog, and actually we're getting a beautiful whippet, could I?" Caitlin's mom came to put her arms around her and Winston and laughed as the puppy scrambled up to lick her, too. "I had to pretend, and it was very difficult. I wanted to tell you so much, especially when I could see how sad you were! I almost gave in and blurted it out, but I thought Dad and Aidan and Lily would never forgive me."

"I still can't believe it," Caitlin replied. "We really have a dog!" It was hard to think of anything with a whippet puppy licking her all over. "Oooh, not in my ear!"

Winston wriggled out from underneath the blanket again and padded across the floor to Caitlin. He didn't want to stay in the basket, even though it was comfortable. If he went to sleep in there, she'd be gone when he woke up—he was sure of it.

He grabbed the blanket in his teeth and yanked at it, pulling it out so that it trailed after him as he padded across to her.

"Hey, didn't you like it in there? I was only getting a drink."

Winston dropped the blanket on her foot and then lay down. He wasn't really sure about this new place and the basket, but Caitlin was the same, and he wasn't letting her get away this time.

He twitched at the blanket, trying to
pull it so that it covered him, but Caitlin
reached down and scooped him up inside
it. Then she sat down next to his basket,
with him on her lap. Winston sniffed
suspiciously at the basket and then
turned around a few times until he was
comfortable. He rested his nose on her
arm so that she couldn't move.

"It's okay," Caitlin whispered,
pulling the blanket a little
tighter around her
puppy. "I'm not going
anywhere. And you're
staying, I promise."

Winston's ears
flickered, but he was
already half asleep.